Copyright © 1993 by Nord-Süd Verlag AG, Gossau Zürich, Switzerland
First published in Switzerland under the title *Die Tiere sind frei!*
English translation copyright © 1993 by Rosemary Lanning

First published in the United States, Great Britain, Canada,
Australia, and New Zealand in 1993 by North-South Books,
an imprint of Nord-Süd Verlag AG, Gossau Zürich, Switzerland.

Distributed in the United States by North-South Books Inc., New York.

Library of Congress Cataloging-in-Publication Data is available.
ISBN 1-55858-201-0 (trade binding)
ISBN 1-55858-202-9 (library binding)

A CIP catalogue record for this book is available
from The British Library.

93-202 1 3 5 7 9 10 8 6 4 2
Printed in Belgium

Escape from the Zoo!

Piotr and Józef Wilkoń

Translated by Rosemary Lanning

North-South Books / New York

It was a warm summer evening at the zoo. All the visitors had gone home, and old Matthew, the zookeeper, had nearly finished work for the day. He was very tired, but there was still one important job to do. He had to check that all the animals were safe and their cages were securely locked.

When, at last, he had completed his rounds, Matthew sat in front of his little house and lit his pipe. He gazed across at his old friend the lion.

"Fast asleep already," he murmured. "Everything is in order." And he, too, drifted off to sleep.

An unexpected noise wakened him. It sounded like the chimpanzees' swing. Matthew jumped up. "It *is* the chimpanzees' swing!" he muttered. There it was, swaying back and forth in an empty cage. The door was unlocked!

Not just that door, but every door! Matthew looked
around and saw that all the cages were empty. Even the
lion was gone. He tried to shout "Help!" but for some
reason he couldn't make a sound. He picked up his keys
and ran to the main gate.

He was just in time to see his animals
disappearing down the narrow streets of the town.
"I must catch them and bring them back,"
gasped Matthew. He ran after the animals as fast
as he could.

Out of breath, Matthew stumbled into a little café. "The animals have escaped!" he shouted, but no one noticed him. He watched helplessly as the rhinoceros stuck its head through the window and noisily gobbled up a small boy's ice cream.

The boy's friend calmly pushed his own bowl of ice cream over to the rhinoceros.

The old zookeeper couldn't believe what he was seeing.

Next Matthew ran after the hippo. He watched aghast as it trotted straight through an open gate, lumbered across a well-kept lawn, then plunged into the swimming pool. The woman sitting beside the pool looked up briefly, flicked a few drops of water from her book, and went on reading.

"What's going on here?" muttered Matthew.

Matthew walked on through the town,
shaking his head in disbelief. Wherever he
looked, he saw more animals from the zoo.
And the strange thing was that no one
seemed surprised or afraid.

The old zookeeper came to a camera shop and peeped through the door. A little girl was posing for her portrait, and right behind her stood the biggest tiger from the zoo, smiling. "Look out!" yelled Matthew.

There was a flash. The girl jumped up and cried: "One more picture! Please take one more picture of me and the dear little tiger!"

The old zookeeper was so bewildered, he didn't even try to catch the tiger, but staggered out into the street and jumped onto the first bus that came along.

Matthew got off the bus when it stopped beside a park overlooking the town. He saw a little girl throwing a yellow ball to her dog. Suddenly, the lion from the zoo jumped out from behind a bush and snatched the ball.

"Give it back!" cried the little girl, holding out her hands.

Matthew tried to shout "Run away!" but not a sound came from his lips.

"What a big cat you are," said the little girl to the lion. "You can keep the ball. Let's go back to my house to play."

It was getting dark. Matthew sat down on a bench. "How tired I am!" he thought. Then he heard a strange noise. Was it the chimpanzees' swing? Yes, it was! A chimpanzee was swinging right above his head, grinning boldly at him and smoking Matthew's pipe. "Now, this really has gone too far!" shouted Matthew. "Give me my pipe!"

"Hoo, hoo, hoo!" chattered the chimpanzee, and the pipe fell from his mouth.

Matthew bent to pick up the pipe, and suddenly he was back outside his own little house. He looked around him. The chimpanzees' swing was still squeaking but the door of the cage was shut, and they were sleeping peacefully on a branch. All the other animals were back where they belonged too.

"Thank goodness!" said Matthew. He got up from his chair and went over to the lion's cage. "It was just a dream, wasn't it, old fellow?" he said, patting the lion on the head. But then something caught Matthew's eye: Lying next to the lion's paw was a little yellow ball. . . .

93-202

E
WIL   Wilkon, Piotr.
            Escape from the zoo!

5901